Six Dinner
Sid

For Richard

First published in 1990
by Simon and Schuster Young Books

This edition published in 2016

Hodder Children's Books
An imprint of Hachette Children's Group
Part of Hodder & Stoughton
Carmelite House
50 Victoria Embankment
London EC4Y 0DZ

A catalogue record of this book is available from the British Library.

ISBN: 978 0 340 89411 8
30

Printed in China

An Hachette UK Company
www.hachette.co.uk

Sid lived at number one, Aristotle Street.

He also lived at number two, number three,
number four, number five and number six.

6
5
4

Sid lived in six houses so that he could have six dinners. Each night he would slip out of number one, where he might have had chicken, into number two for fish…

on to number three for lamb,

mince at number four,

fish again at number five…

rounding off at number six
with beef and kidney stew.

Since no one talked to their neighbours
in Aristotle Street, no one knew what
Sid was up to. They each believed
the cat they fed was theirs,
and theirs alone.

But Sid had to work hard for his dinners. It wasn't easy being six people's pet. He had six different names to remember and six different ways to behave.

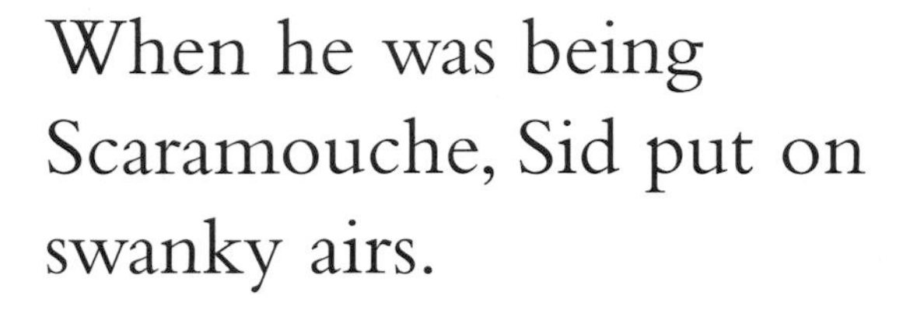

When he was being Scaramouche, Sid put on swanky airs.

As Bob he had a job.

He was naughty as Satan…

and silly as Sally.

As Sooty he smooched…

but as Schwartz he had to act rough and tough.

All this work sometimes
wore Sid out. But he
didn't care, as long as
he had his six dinners.
And, besides, he
liked being…

scratched in six different places…

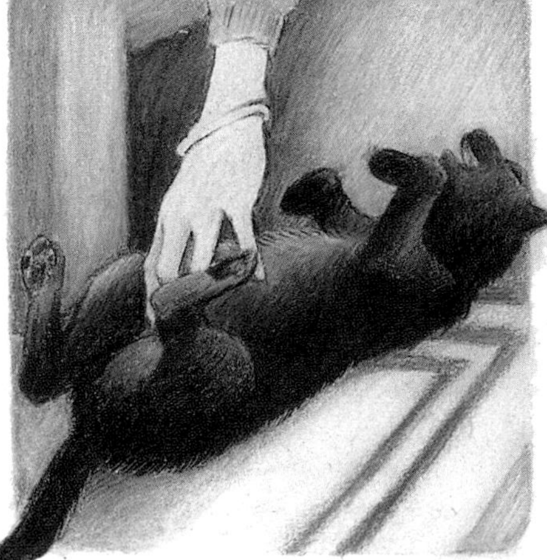

and sleeping in six different beds.

In fact, life in
Aristotle Street
was just about
perfect for Sid,
until…

one cold damp day, he caught a nasty cough.

The next thing he knew,
he was being taken to see the vet.
Poor Sid, he was taken not once…

not twice…

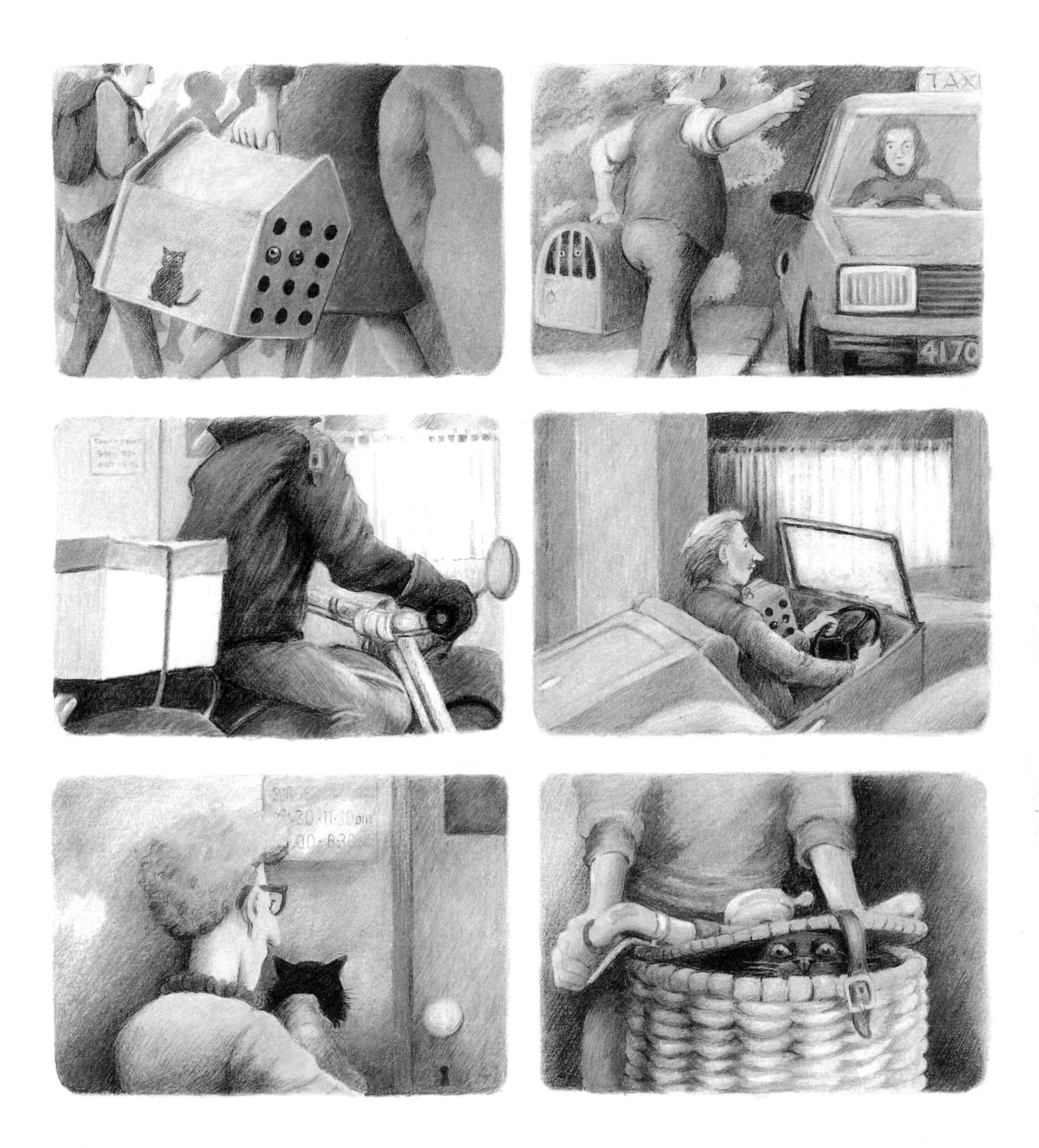

but six times!
He went with six different people,
in six different ways.

The vet said Sid's cough wasn't nearly as nasty as it sounded, but, to be on the safe side, he should have a spoonful of medicine.

Of course, Sid didn't have
just one spoonful of
medicine.

He had six!

Now, one black cat does look much like another, but nobody, not even a busy vet, could see the same cat six times without becoming suspicious. Sure enough, when he checked in his appointment book, the vet found six cats with a cough – all living in Aristotle Street!

So he rang the owners at once…

and, oh dear, Sid was found out!
When they discovered what he had been up to,
Sid's owners were furious. They said he had
no business eating so many dinners.

They said, in future, they would make sure
he had only one dinner a day.

PYTHAGORAS
PLACE

But Sid was a six-dinner-a-day cat.
So he went to live at number one, Pythagoras Place.
He also went to live at numbers two, three, four,
five and six.

Unlike Aristotle Street, the people
who lived in Pythagoras Place
talked to their neighbours.
So, right from the start,
everyone knew about
Sid's six dinners.

And, because everyone knew,
nobody minded.